JUMANJI

Written and Illustrated by CHRIS VAN ALLSBURG

ANDERSEN PRESS

To Tom S.

Thanks to Michaela, Allison, and Ruth

This paperback edition published in 2017 by Andersen Press Ltd.
First published in USA in 1981 by Houghton Mifflin Harcourt Publishing Company.

Published by special arrangement with Houghton Mifflin Harcourt Publishing Company,
and Rights People, London.

The rights of Chris Van Allsburg to be identified as the author and illustrator of this work
have been asserted by him in accordance with the Copyright, Designs and Patents Act, 1988.
Printed and bound in Malaysia.

7   9   10   8   6

British Library Cataloguing in Publication Data available.

ISBN 978 1 78344 676 6

JUMANJI

"Now remember," Mother said, "your father and I are bringing some guests by after the opera, so please keep the house neat."

"Quite so," added Father, tucking his scarf inside his coat.

Mother peered into the hall mirror and carefully pinned her hat in place, then knelt and kissed both children goodbye.

When the front door closed, Judy and Peter giggled with delight. They took all the toys out of their toy chest and made a terrible mess. But their laughter slowly turned to silence till finally Peter slouched into a chair.

"You know what?" he said. "I'm really bored."

"Me too," sighed Judy. "Why don't we go outside and play?"

Peter agreed, so they set off across the street to the park. It was cold for November. The children could see their breath like steam. They rolled in the leaves and when Judy tried to stuff some leaves down Peter's sweater he jumped up and ran behind a tree.

When his sister caught up with him, he was kneeling at the foot of the tree, looking at a long thin box.

"What's that?" Judy asked.

"It's a game," said Peter, handing her the box.

"'JUMANJI,'" Judy read from the box, "'A JUNGLE ADVENTURE GAME.'"

"Look," said Peter, pointing to a note taped to the bottom of the box. In a childlike handwriting were the words "Free game, fun for some but not for all. P.S. Read instructions carefully."

"Want to take it home?" Judy asked.

"Not really," said Peter. "I'm sure somebody left it here because it's so boring."

"Oh, come on," protested Judy. "Let's give it a try. Race you home!" And off she ran with Peter at her heels.

At home, the children spread the game out on a card table. It looked very much like the games they already had. There was a board that unfolded, revealing a path of coloured squares. The squares had messages written on them. The path started in the deepest jungle and ended up in Jumanji, a city of golden buildings and towers. Peter began to shake the dice and play with the other pieces that were in the box.

"Put those down and listen," said Judy. "I'm going to read the instructions: 'Jumanji, a young people's jungle adventure especially designed for the bored and restless.

"'A. Player selects piece and places it in deepest jungle. B. Player rolls dice and moves piece along path through the dangers of the jungle. C. First player to reach Jumanji and yell the city's name aloud is the winner.'"

"Is that all?" asked Peter, sounding disappointed.

"No," said Judy, "there's one more thing, and this is in capital letters: 'D. VERY IMPORTANT: ONCE A GAME OF JUMANJI IS STARTED IT WILL NOT BE OVER UNTIL ONE PLAYER REACHES THE GOLDEN CITY.'"

"Oh, big deal," said Peter, who gave a bored yawn.

"Here," said Judy, handing her brother the dice, "you go first."

Peter casually dropped the dice from his hand.

"Seven," said Judy.

Peter moved his piece to the seventh square.

"'Lion attacks, move back two spaces,'" read Judy.

"Gosh, how exciting," said Peter, in a very unexcited voice. As he reached for his piece he looked up at his sister. She had a look of absolute horror on her face.

"Peter," she whispered, "turn around very, very slowly."

The boy turned in his chair. He couldn't believe his eyes. Lying on the piano was a lion, staring at Peter and licking his lips.

The lion roared so loud it knocked Peter right off his chair. The big cat jumped to the floor. Peter was up on his feet, running through the house with the lion a whisker's length behind. He ran upstairs and dived under a bed. The lion tried to squeeze under, but got his head stuck. Peter scrambled out, ran from the bedroom, and slammed the door behind him. He stood in the hall with Judy, gasping for breath.

"I don't think," said Peter in between gasps of air, "that I want… to play… this game… any more."

"But we have to," said Judy as she helped Peter back downstairs. "I'm sure that's what the instructions mean. That lion won't go away until one of us wins the game."

Peter stood next to the card table. "Can't we just call the zoo and have him taken away?" From upstairs came the sounds of growling and clawing at the bedroom door. "Or maybe we could wait till Father comes home."

"No one would come from the zoo because they wouldn't believe us," said Judy. "And you know how upset Mother would be if there was a lion in the bedroom. We started this game, and now we have to finish it."

Peter looked down at the game board. What if Judy rolled a seven? Then there'd be two lions. For an instant Peter thought he was going to cry. Then he sat firmly in his chair and said, "Let's play."

Judy picked up the dice, rolled an eight, and moved her piece.

"'Monkeys steal food, miss one turn,'" she read. From the kitchen came the sounds of banging pots and falling jars. The children ran in to see a dozen monkeys tearing the room apart.

"Oh boy," said Peter, "this would upset Mother even more than the lion."

"Quick," said Judy, "back to the game."

Peter took his turn. Thank heavens, he landed on a blank space. He rolled again. "'Monsoon season begins, lose one turn.'" Little raindrops began to fall in the living room. Then a roll of thunder shook the walls and scared the monkeys out of the kitchen. The rain began to fall in buckets as Judy took the dice.

"'Guide gets lost, lose one turn.'" The rain suddenly stopped. The children turned to see a man hunched over a map.

"Oh dear, I say, spot of bad luck now," he mumbled.

"Perhaps a left turn here then… No, no… a right turn here… Yes, absolutely, I think, a right turn… or maybe…"

"Excuse me," said Judy, but the guide just ignored her.

"…around here, then over… No, no… over here and around this… Yes, good… but then… Hm…"

Judy shrugged her shoulders and handed the dice to Peter.

"...four, five, six," he counted. " 'Bitten by tsetse fly, contract sleeping sickness, lose one turn.' "

Judy heard a faint buzzing noise and watched a small insect land on Peter's nose. Peter lifted his hand to brush the bug away, but then stopped, gave a tremendous yawn, and fell sound asleep, his head on the table.

"Peter, Peter, wake up!" cried Judy. But it was no use. She grabbed the dice and moved to a blank. She rolled again and waited in amazement. "'Rhinoceros stampede, go back two spaces.'"

As fast as he had fallen asleep, Peter awoke. Together they listened to a rumble in the hallway. It grew louder and louder. Suddenly a herd of rhinos charged through the living room and into the dining room, crushing all the furniture in their path. Peter and Judy covered their ears as sounds of splintering wood and breaking china filled the house.

Peter gave the dice a quick tumble. "'Python sneaks into camp, go back one space.'"

Judy shrieked and jumped up on her chair.

"Over the fireplace," said Peter. Judy sat down again, nervously eyeing the eight-foot snake that was wrapping itself around the mantel clock. The guide looked up from his map, took one look at the snake, and moved to the far corner of the room, joining the monkeys on the couch.

Judy took her turn and landed on a blank space. Her brother took the dice and rolled a three.

"Oh, no," he moaned. "'Volcano erupts, go back three spaces.'" The room became warm and started to shake a little. Molten lava poured from the fireplace opening. It hit the water on the floor and the room filled with steam. Judy rolled the dice and moved ahead.

"'Discover shortcut, roll again.' Oh dear!" she cried. Judy saw the snake unwrapping himself from the clock.

"If you roll a twelve you can get out of the jungle," said Peter.

"Please, please," Judy begged as she shook the dice. The snake was wriggling his way to the floor. She dropped the dice from her hand. One six, then another. Judy grabbed her piece and slammed it to the board. "**JUMANJI**," she yelled, as loud as she could.

The steam in the room became thicker and thicker. Judy could not even see Peter across the table. Then, as if all the doors and windows had been opened, a cool breeze cleared the steam from the room. Everything was just as it had been before the game. No monkeys, no guide, no water, no broken furniture, no snake, no lion roaring upstairs, no rhinos. Without saying a word to each other, Peter and Judy threw the game into its box.

They bolted out of the door, ran across the street to the park, and dropped the game under a tree. Back home, they quickly put all their toys away. But both children were too excited to sit quietly, so Peter took out a picture puzzle. As they fit the pieces together, their excitement slowly turned to relief, and then exhaustion. With the puzzle half done Peter and Judy fell sound asleep on the sofa.

"Wake up, dears," Mother's voice called.

Judy opened her eyes. Mother and Father had returned and their guests were arriving. Judy gave Peter a nudge to wake him. Yawning and stretching, they got to their feet.

Mother introduced them to some of the guests, then asked, "Did you have an exciting afternoon?"

"Oh yes," said Peter. "We had a flood, a stampede, a volcano, I got sleeping sickness, and—" Peter was interrupted by the adults' laughter.

"Well," said Mother, "I think you both got sleeping sickness. Why don't you go upstairs and put your pyjamas on? Then you can finish your puzzle and have some dinner."

When Peter and Judy came back downstairs they found that Father had moved the puzzle into the den. While the children were working on it, one of the guests, Mrs Budwing, brought them a tray of food.

"Such a hard puzzle," she said to the children. "Daniel and Walter are always starting puzzles and never finishing them." Daniel and Walter were Mrs Budwing's sons. "They never read instructions either. Oh well," said Mrs Budwing, turning to rejoin the guests, "I guess they'll learn."

Both children answered, "I hope so," but they weren't looking at Mrs Budwing. They were looking out of the window. Two boys were running through the park. They were Danny and Walter Budwing, and Danny had a long, thin box under his arm.

Other books by
CHRIS VAN ALLSBURG

Queen of the Falls
9781849392723

The Mysteries of Harris Burdick
9781849392792

The Polar Express
9781842709498

The Polar Express Book and CD
9781849390989

The Chronicles of Harris Burdick
9781849394086